AF010979

THE
LITTLE
BOOK
OF

Trolls

THE
LITTLE
BOOK
OF

Trolls

Carolyne Larrington

BRITISH LIBRARY

First published in 2025 by
The British Library
96 Euston Road
London NW1 2DB

ISBN 978 0 7123 5518 6

Cataloguing-in Publication Data
A catalogue record for this book is available from the
British Library

Title page: All the trolls burst into a fit of laughter, from
'The Golden Bird', illustrated by Theodor Kittelsen, 1882.

Designed and typeset by Georgie Hewitt
Picture Research by Sally Nicholls

Printed and bound in the Czech Republic by PBTisk

For product safety information, please visit shop.bl.uk/pages/
british-library-publishing, or the Publishing pages on bl.uk.

CONTENTS

HVEM ER DE
SOM TRAMPER
PAA
G. Munthe.

INTRODUCTION

What is a troll? The short answer is a Scandinavian folkloric being, usually imagined as very large, ugly and malign, living in the wilderness, but interacting with humans for various reasons. Trolls have a long history, dating back to the earliest Old Norse poetry, recorded in Iceland in the medieval period. They continued to play a key role in folklore, featuring in oral tales passed on in rural communities; these stories served to warn about the dangers that might befall humans in the forests and mountains, but they also provided entertainment, and offered an assurance that those perils could be overcome through human quick-wittedness. In the nineteenth century, folktales and ballads about trolls began to be collected and published across Scandinavia. These were very soon translated into a range of other languages, bringing the concept of the troll into English, through the hugely popular story of 'The Three Billy Goats Gruff.' Over the past two hundred years their fame – or notoriety – has grown, taking on new meanings within global popular culture.

'Who's that crossing MY bridge?' asks the fearsome troll in Gerhard Munthe's 1908 watercolour of 'Three Billy Goats Gruff'.

Trolls come in many shapes and sizes. Some are taller than trees and the ground trembles as they approach. Some indeed are so huge that they appear to be mountains and go unnoticed by humans until they open an eye. Other trolls vary in size, so that they interact with humans on the same level. Although their main habitats are the forests and mountains of Norway and Sweden, the rolling pastures of Denmark, or Iceland's bleak and forbidding desert interior, there are also sea-trolls who surface to menace the unwary fisherman. Not all trolls are nasty, though a good number of them eat humans when they can catch them. Others can be friendly and helpful, and they usually keep the promises that they make to people. There are male and female trolls; male trolls seem often to prefer human women, especially princesses, as partners, but there are some troll-mothers in the stories who love their ugly offspring with a powerful maternal passion. Trolls might sometimes be quite cunning, but they do not necessarily think things through, and thus the smart human will manage to outwit them by the story's end.

Where Do We Find Troll Stories?

Most of the tales we have about trolls were collected in the nineteenth century from rural folk in different parts of Scandinavia

A slumbering troll awakens in a 1906 drawing by Theodor Kittelsen.

Overleaf: A troll about to stamp on unsuspecting travellers in an 1896 painting by Christian Skredsvig.

Dunderdingsen
og Dingelingsen
96.

The cover of the 1874 edition of Peter Christen Asbjørnsen and Jørgen Moe's *Norske folkeeventyr* (Norwegian Folktales).

and Iceland. The best-known stories are the Norwegian ones, collected by Peter Christen Asbjørnsen and Jørgen Moe and first published in Norway in 1843–4. Asbjørnsen and Moe were inspired by the fairy- and folktales collections of the Brothers Grimm in Germany. Swedish and Danish collectors included Eva Wigström, working in the late 1880s, and Frederik Lange Grundtvig, who researched into the survival of Danish folklore among emigrants to America in the 1880s and 1890s. In Iceland, Jón Árnason brought together the slightly different and rather quirky Icelandic folktales; these were mostly published in the 1860s. These collections played an important part in the construction of national identity, particularly in Norway and Iceland, which were subordinate to the Danish crown at that time. Asbjørnsen and Moe's collections, often reprinted, motivated others to gather up rural tales, and even to compose their own original stories of trolls, giants, witches and princesses. The Swedish annual *Bland Tomtar och Troll* (Among Brownies and Trolls), which began in 1907 and is still published yearly, contains many such tales, based on folk motifs. The stories, new and old, inspired some of the most talented artists and illustrators of the day. The Norwegian Theodor Kittelsen (1857–1914) is especially famous for his troll illustrations, while the Swedish John Bauer (1882–1918), who died tragically young, illustrated many issues of *Bland Tomtar och Troll*, and brought his unique vision to other original story collections.

This book will introduce you to a whole range of trolls, from the earliest medieval trolls, via the many trolls of folklore, legend and fairytale to the modern reflexes of the troll. They can be found in

The illustrated title page of *Legends of Iceland*, folktales collected by Jón Árnason, translated by George E. J. Powell and Eiríkur Magnússon in 1864.

The cover of the inaugural 1907 issue of *Bland Tomtar och Troll* (Among Brownies and Trolls), the iconic Swedish folklore annual.

contemporary culture as positive figures: as cute collectables, or lovable stars of children's animated films. In recent movies, they have symbolised natural predators, environmental protestors or minorities in mainstream society; in fantasy literature they form an underclass which challenges existing social institutions. Their most familiar habitat is, however, in social media where they lurk in the shadows of anonymity, embodying negativity, charmlessness and, sometimes, genuine threat. Trolls have expanded a long way from their Scandinavian homeland, not least on the internet, and they function as significant figures in contemporary imaginations.

e
nd Islands
e TROWS
are similiar
Scandinavian
and, like them,
an aversion
ylight.
are frequently
ved
nning a
us lop-sided
e called
king

THE EARLIEST TROLLS

We first find trolls in medieval sagas and poems that are often set in mainland Scandinavia, but which were first written down in thirteenth- and fourteenth-century Iceland. These supernatural figures clearly migrated to the island with the Norwegians who settled it in the ninth and tenth centuries; other Scandinavian migrants came to the British Isles in the medieval period, bringing their belief systems with them. The trows of Shetland, for example, have some similarities with the Scandinavian trolls; they can be very big and sometimes three-headed, but the folklore of the Northern Isles usually casts trows rather as fairy-like and quite small. They are prone to stealing children and women and are very fond of fiddle music and dancing.

The word *troll* in Old Norse, the medieval language of Scandinavia, has a much wider application than it does in modern English, for the primary meaning of the *troll*-root is 'magic', and *troll* (or *trold* in

A mischievous Northern Isles trow, as imagined by Brian Froud.

Danish) still has that meaning in modern Scandinavian languages. In Old Norse, the noun *troll* could be applied to a range of creatures that could also be referred to as *jötnar* (often translated as 'giants') or *flögð*, singular *flagð*, 'ogresses.' (The letter ð is pronounced like the 'th' in 'that.') *Trolldómr* meant 'magic, magical practices' and the verb *trylla*, 'to bewitch.' A common curse in the sagas is 'may the trolls take you!', the equivalent of 'go to hell!' But generally, except when someone is insulting another person by calling them a troll, sagas and poems have a clear idea of the kind of creatures that the word refers to: at least human-size and generally larger, ugly and hostile, capable both of speech and of cunning and with very clear agendas of their own.

Ketill, Grímr and the Trolls

Trolls usually live away from human habitation, in the deserted Icelandic interior and in caverns high up in the mountains. In stories set in mainland Scandinavia they have ramshackle dwellings or cave-homes deep in the forest. They generally keep out of humans' way but react angrily to what they see as trespass into their territory. They also raid farms and snatch animals and people for food. One legendary Icelandic saga gives a gruesome account of storage pits found by a hero called Ketill. These are full of salted meat, seal, polar bear, walrus ... and at the bottom of each pit Ketill discovers human meat. He promptly sabotages the meat-store and tosses its contents away in disgust. In some sagas, the lineage of a hero can be traced back to *jötnar*, trolls or trollish figures; indeed,

Ketill has a father called Hallbjörn halftroll. The disgruntled owner of the meat-storage pits notes that Hallbjörn is his friend and it is most likely Hallbjörn's no-good son Ketill who has ruined his food supply. Ketill himself stays the winter with someone called Bruni and sleeps with his daughter, Hrafnhildur, described by the saga-writer as 'big and splendid.' What kind of creature Bruni might be is not specified, but after Ketill returns home, Hrafnhildur comes to visit, bringing their little son. Hallbjörn rudely demands to know who has invited this troll to his house; clearly, marriage between Ketill and Hrafnhildur is impossible and she departs, bitterly unhappy. Both Ketill and Grímr, his son, encounter troll-women in their adventures in the Norwegian north and usually kill them with ease, since Ketill is equipped with magic arrows, provided by Bruni's brother. Indeed, in his own saga Grímr finds himself in bed with a hideous troll-girl whom he has to kiss. He falls asleep by her side, but awakens to find that she has transformed herself into his beautiful missing fiancée. Her wicked stepmother had turned her into a troll, and her troll-skin lies discarded nearby.

Sea-Troll-Women

On his first adventure in the far north, Ketill is on board his boat, when a huge storm blows up. Then something takes hold of the stern of his boat and shakes it violently. This proves to be a troll-woman; Ketill manages to make his escape, partly because Bruni, in the shape of a whale, magically protects him. Troll-women are a considerable hazard in the maritime landscape as well as on shore.

atta. at. mu- þ leg ... m por ...
tetin e adal ure at þu mun ala bg v sidu m e þu meett vt a
la bg v þ er bglozin e j allar cetr. þ plum miog þm red sig
dar z gek h at ceiga attu. Sigdr v halpd. s. sigd s. hrisa hr. son
hins harpagra. sigdr syr uar spekingr mikill gopugr m z a
udigr en ceinge uar h hinads. en kostiosu m v h godr red
ar z hops mads um alla hluti. pceddizt ol. nu upp m; sigd
stiup podur sinu z astu mod sine þ mentu olaps kgs. cap.

Olapr ht. son v sueina gaulugr m pos synu medal m
ueysti. vart v h suema z ecd smalir. Sigdr kr v bu
sysslu m mikill z hapde m sinar miog s stiupsun z h
sealpr pos oprliga at sea v akra sina eds ceing eds penat
eds en e smida e þ sem m storpudu ceir huar. þ v ceit sin
et. s. kr uillde ridat ap stad e þa v ceigem. condr laus. hn
buadde þa ol stiup son sin t at taka a hert z saudla. ol. gek
vt til geita hus z tok bukk þn e mestr v z leidde hei z lagde
a sodulreide kgs. gek þa z sagde hm at h hapde buit hm rei
dskiota þa gek s. kr z sa huat ol. hapde gt. h m þa. audset
er þ at þu uillt ap þ venia budding minar. ed hui pebeu m
þna reidskiota. ol. su. sart s sub m va kr þur hea odr kgm
sem reidskiote þn e hea hestu þ ridder hapa s vehi du. s. su
þ synizt s þu at v eru ollkaplik Alfa gaf ol sudr bæsingh

Pat er ol. v vij uetra gamall var h ollu m vigu sinu
ictrni olldr olikr saber urt z allrar atgiru sua ber tel
oem hun nund er atta mod hs lauk upp hudzslu sine
oemie þa sa suemi at biart v norbir et botnu. ol spurde h
uar þ v þ eru sudr hiollr q atta. hin e q ol. þu ert sour min
sagde h þ e sud er besingr hett z hep at ol. geurttada alpr
ek uil hapa q ol. z m; þa. atta sellde hm sudit z pr h m; z por
ti. s. kgi oc v dat ol m; þr þ þ at h ute h epr hellar golpin en
sudit miog buit. sigurdr geord ... v attu at þ se edli kena at la
at þ uir epr komu er parplegra e e þeu þr tast bur e parp atta

In one Norse poem, the sea-going hero Helgi kills a troll called Hati; as night falls, Helgi bunks down on his ship. The troll's daughter, Hrímgerðr, appears and challenges the ship's watchman, Atli. She demands compensation for her father, and exchanges insults with Atli, admitting that she would have sunk all Helgi's ships if they had not been protected by the hero's lover, the Valkyrie Sigrún. Hrímgerðr demands to spend the night with Helgi as redress for her father's death, but the sun rises while they are still arguing. Helgi cries in triumph:

> 'It's day now, Hrímgerðr,
> Atli has kept you talking
> until you laid down your life;
> you look laughable,
> standing there
> transformed into stone.'

Trolls are generally nocturnal creatures, so careless Hrímgerðr meets the traditional fate of trolls upon whom the sun shines: she becomes a rocky harbour-marker in the fjord over which she once ruled.

A female sea-troll is vanquished by the valiant hero in *Flateyjarbók*, a fourteenth-century manuscript from medieval Iceland containing several sagas.

Arinnefja the Troll-Queen

The sagas often depict trolls as living with their families in caves, but this does not mean that they have no other social organisation. As we will see later, trolls are usually ruled over by a king, and in one Icelandic legendary saga we hear about a female figure, Arinnefja, who aspires to be queen of Jötunheimar (Giantlands). She was once very beautiful – enough to have had an affair with the god Thor – but has lost her looks for complicated reasons and is now at war with her uncles. They have stolen the treasures she has inherited from her parents and have usurped her right to rule over Jötunheimar. Arinnefja and her troll-daughter encounter two human heroes roaming in the wilderness near their home; the men are searching for two kidnapped princesses. Arinnefja knows that her uncles are behind the kidnap and agrees to help the men to rescue the princesses before they are forced to marry their abductors; this will further her plan to regain her kingdom. Before the weddings, the two troll-uncles call an assembly to decide which brother shall rule over the kingdom. Skröggr, the assembly's lawspeaker (the person who knows, recites and applies all the society's laws), is in cahoots with Arinnefja, aiding her and the heroes to infiltrate the wedding in troll disguise. The wedding is a very jolly affair; the disconsolate brides cheer up mightily when Arinnefja whispers to them that rescue is at hand, and the bridegrooms become much happier once their brides are no longer moping. A huge number of troll guests are present at the feast, and there is plenty to eat and drink, as well as music and dancing. When it is time for the couples to go to bed, Arinnefja arranges for the brides to be spirited away in a magic carpet, while the men kill the bridegrooms. Skröggr the lawspeaker alone slays ninety trolls, granting terms to those who are willing to accept Arinnefja's rule. In the end, Arinnefja regains her realm, with Skröggr as her chief counsellor and lover, while the heroes of course marry the princesses. Arinnefja and her daughter are honoured wedding guests; when the party ends, they are sent away with gifts that are desirable in Jötunheimar: an enormous trough full of butter and two sizeable flitches of bacon. Arinnefja, we are told, thought these treasures were better than their equivalent weight in gold (of which she already has plenty at home).

This saga has a strong streak of comedy mixed into the heroic adventures, and it's likely that the figure of Arinnefja the troll-queen represents a satirical Icelandic comment on Queen Margrethe I, who ruled over Norway, Denmark and Sweden at the time of its composition (the late fourteenth century). The trolls are envisaged as living within a society that parallels that of humans; they decorate their cave-palace splendidly for the wedding and arrange for ornate bridal beds and vast amounts of food. That they should also hold a general assembly to determine who shall rule over them underlines the tale's political subtext.

Grettir and the Trolls

There are many more medieval troll-adventures in the sagas; even in relatively late ones, composed in the fifteenth century, trolls figure as potent menaces. Whether contemporary Icelanders really believed in such figures is a moot question. In one of the best-known sagas of that century, *Grettir's saga*, the young man Grettir is travelling with a party across the Icelandic interior, on his way to the Althing (general assembly). He falls out with Skeggi, one of the servants; lagging behind the main group, the men come to blows and Grettir kills Skeggi with his axe. When the others ask what has happened, Grettir recites a verse in which he claims that a troll-woman attacked the victim. The men comment that it's surprising that a troll should attack in broad daylight, but their leader, a high-status chieftain, knows that in poetic convention axes can be described with metaphors connected with troll-women. He decodes Grettir's verse and declares that Grettir is the assailant and his axe the murder weapon. Grettir admits his responsibility and is temporarily outlawed for Skeggi's killing when they arrive at the assembly.

Later in the saga, Grettir is involved in a terrible incident in Norway. He is mistaken for a troll, attacked by a group of Icelanders and, in defending himself, accidentally burns down a hall, causing many fatalities. He is condemned to permanent outlawry in Iceland, and wanders from place to place, seeking shelter. Thus, he comes to a farm plagued by troll attack every Christmas Eve. While others take refuge elsewhere, Grettir waits up for the trolls. At midnight a troll-woman enters the farmhouse and they wrestle fiercely. Grettir is dragged outside to the edge of a nearby ravine and the troll-woman tries to hurl him down into it. Finally, he manages to get a hand free, grab her knife and cut off her arm at the shoulder. The troll-woman plunges into the ravine; worn out, Grettir staggers

The outlaw hero Grettir is ready to fight in a seventeenth-century Icelandic manuscript.

home. That's one of the trolls dealt with, but the valley-folk know there are two of them. The local priest refuses to believe Grettir's story and is recruited to aid him in exploring the ravine after Christmas. The priest is to keep watch over a rope and haul Grettir up after his reconnaissance of the trolls' lair. Grettir leaps down into the ravine and climbs up behind a powerful waterfall where there is a cave. There he finds a *jötunn* sitting by a fire, who attacks him. Grettir kills the troll with his own sword, hanging in the cave, but when the priest sees the creature's guts floating in the river, he concludes that Grettir is dead and goes home. Grettir explores the cave, finding treasure and human bones which he puts into a bag to bring back with him. When he reaches the bottom of the rope, no one is there to draw him up; poor Grettir must climb hand over hand out of the ravine after his exhausting adventure. The bones are given Christian burial and the priest apologises handsomely to Grettir. No more untoward supernatural events occur in the valley after that: Grettir has cleansed the place.

Shape-Changing Troll-Women

A number of sagas and ballads feature wicked stepmothers, often with daughters, who seduce and marry widowed kings. The stepmother works to alienate the king from his son and heir; sometimes she just wants to cut him out of his inheritance so

Grettir overcomes the troll-woman, who plunges into the ravine, in John Vernon Lord's illustration for the 2002 Folio Society edition of *Icelandic Sagas*.

that her own child can take the throne, but in other stories the stepmother makes sexual advances to her younger and more handsome stepson. She deploys not only her beauty and charm, but often trollish magic, to try to seduce him; when he rebuffs her, she becomes a dangerous enemy. In one story the unfortunate hero is turned into a wolf and is rescued from his condition only after much suffering. The stepmother is always finally revealed as the troll she really is, and thoroughly merits her eventual unmasking and annihilation. As we'll see later, in the twentieth-century Swedish tale, 'The Adventure', a princess is abducted by trolls with the connivance of her secretly trollish stepmother, so that the new queen's own daughter can take the princess's place.

The evidence from Norse sagas and poetry points to a complex picture of trolls as not easily distinguished from *jötnar* or giants, or other terms for human-size or larger supernatural creatures. Trolls tend not to identify themselves as trolls; it's the narrators or heroes who call them by that name. Many are terrifying and monstrous, dwelling far from human habitation and attacking those who venture into their territory; these are the ones who eat human flesh, but others can be more friendly to humans, affording them food and shelter and even inviting them to have sexual relationships with their daughters. Troll-women cannot be allowed to marry humans, however loving the relationship, but this does not prevent children born with troll blood becoming significant ancestors within the family lineage. Although many troll-women are savage and dangerous, some, like Arinnefja, become patrons of human heroes, ready to help them in battle, to give them magical gifts, or to devise complex strategies to help their young friends achieve their aims. Medieval trolls, then, have all the hallmarks of their folkloric descendants, but they often embody more positive qualities than later trolls, including physical attractiveness and the capacity to form loving, long-lasting relationships with humans.

Th. Kittelsen

KINDLY TROLLS

We have seen that medieval trolls can be well intentioned towards humans, offering them shelter over the winter, becoming romantically involved with them or taking on supportive roles. The trolls of Scandinavian folklore are not generally so pleasant, but there are some tales of positive interactions. In Sweden and Denmark there are stories of trolls who come to human houses, wanting to borrow provisions. They may have run out of meal for their porridge, or in one tale from Jutland, in Denmark, a troll wedding is on the horizon and the trolls don't have enough beer. An ugly little troll approaches a farmer's wife and asks if he can borrow a barrel of beer if he brings back an equivalent just as good in a few days' time. The transaction is complicated by the fact that all the farm's barrels have crosses marked on the top – to keep them safe from trolls, of course – but the wife scratches off the cross and the troll carries it away. Sure enough, he returns a few days later with a barrel of equal size; the beer in it turns out to be excellent and the farm has good fortune from that day

An elderly female troll enjoys her brimming porridge dish, illustrated by Theodor Kittelsen in 1900.

In this 1882 illustration by Theodor Kittelsen a headless troll-woman politely asks a mother if her son is at home.

onwards. This kind of tale, about fair exchange and help among neighbours, has many parallels in European folklore; in Scotland it is often the fairies who come looking for a temporary loan. If you don't feel like lending your resources to trolls, ill luck can overtake you. Trolls know when they are being lied to about your own lack of provisions and you will indeed find that your cow has now stopped giving milk and your beer has soured in the barrel.

Grateful Trolls

Grateful trolls are rare, but in one story from Iceland a young man is riding to the school at Skálholt, one of the country's two dioceses, along with seventeen friends – the autumn term has started. As they cross the glacial sands on the island's south coast, they spot a creature 'like a human' going along on all fours. They realise it's a troll-woman. She calls out, asking for help to get over the glacial river, but they laugh at her and ride on. The last lad in the party, though, Thórarinn, takes pity on her and lets her jump up behind him on the horse. Now she's able to follow the river back home, and she advises Thórarinn exactly where to leave his horses at pasture when he gets to Skálholt. The winter is very hard and when the boys round up their horses to go home for the summer, everyone else's horses are emaciated and unfit for the journey. They have to buy new ones. Thórarinn's horses are in splendid condition, even fatter than they were in the autumn: a troll reward. Later in life, Thórarinn, now a priest, is in great danger when, travelling in the interior, he and a boy are caught in a sudden blizzard. Not only does

Peder Lars's horse is sped onwards by the grateful troll-woman in 'The Troll Ride' (1910), illustrated by John Bauer.

Running late, Peder Lars's horse is spurred on by the help of the troll-woman in 'The Troll Ride', by John Bauer.

his troll-friend rescue them, she and her daughter invite them into their comfortable cave-home, for the troll-woman was pregnant when she asked for his help all those years earlier and that was why she needed his assistance. When the weather improves, they direct their guests to the route home; the troll-woman asks only that Thórarinn might send her something to eat. So he has twenty old sheep and an eight-year-old ox driven up-valley and the two remain friends all their lives.

A modern story by Anna Wahlenberg, 'Troll Ritt' (The Troll Ride), takes up the same theme. Peder Lars is rushing to present his marriage suit to the beautiful Lisa; he must be at her home by six in the evening or she will marry another. He hears a voice calling out to him from the ditch; a troll-woman has injured her leg and needs resin from the pine trees in the nearby woods to heal her. At first Peder Lars refuses – he is in too much of a hurry. Then he hears the troll's mother singing sadly, calling for her daughter, 'sweet and fair'; the song haunts him as he tries to ride on. Finally, he turns back and fetches the resin, even though he is sure it will cost him his beloved. As his horse races onwards to Lisa's house, Peder Lars feels as if something is sitting behind him and he reaches his destination just as the clock strikes the hour: his suit is accepted. Thereafter, even if Peder Lars were late setting out on an errand, somehow, he would always arrive on time; the troll-woman would jump up behind him to speed the horse on. Despite Peder Lars's doubts about the creature, 'it was an honest troll, and he certainly did receive a reward', the story notes.

Why You Should Do What Trolls Tell You

A well-known Norwegian tale recounts an instance of troll assistance that went badly wrong. At Vaage in the Gudbrandsdal valley there is a mountain called Jutulsberg (Giant's Mountain), and on one side of it is a rock formation that looks like a huge gateway. In the old days, if you wanted to borrow something from the trolls, you could go to the gateway, toss a stone at it and cry, 'Open, Jutul' and the inhabitant might or might not answer his door. Johannes Blessom from Blessom farm in the valley is in far-off Copenhagen, trying to get justice in a lawsuit. Christmas Eve comes and the case is over; Johannes is desperate to get home, but knows that he has many days journeying ahead. Suddenly, a man wearing the costume of his own native parish of Vaage hurries past him in the street: a tall man whose shirt has huge silver buttons. Johannes thinks he knows him, but can't quite see his face, so he hails him. The stranger says he will be back in Vaage that very night and offers Johannes a lift: his horse can cover a Norwegian mile (about ten kilometres) in twelve strides and Johannes can stand on the sledge's back runner. Johannes gratefully accepts. During the journey, Johannes can see neither earth nor sky; they travel in a sinister space between the worlds. When they stop for a brief rest, he spots a skull mounted on a pole. Now they are almost home, at the bridge over the Finna river. The driver drops Johannes off and tells him not to look round if he hears a rumbling sound or senses a strange light behind him. Of course, Johannes disobeys, looks

P.N.Arbo

Johannes Blessom takes an unearthly lift with a troll to get home in a single night, illustrated by Peter Nicolai Arbo in 1879.

round and sees the mountain open up with the light of a thousand candles blazing within and the troll or giant striding inside. In punishment, Johannes's head sat crookedly on his neck for the rest of his days. As in other folktales about supernatural creatures who do humans a favour, it is vital to follow their instructions to the letter or some disaster will undoubtedly befall you.

Amorous Trolls

Troll-women can be very friendly to good-looking, or even not so good-looking, men. Several stories from Sweden and Norway tell of strange women who emerge from the forest to befriend a man. Charcoal Nils has a farm but makes his living from charcoal-burning. He cannot produce enough to prosper until, one day, a woman offers to help him; she drags so much wood to his kiln that he can make large amounts of high-quality charcoal. She lives with him as his wife for a while, and they have three children. She now begins to demand that they go to live at his farm, but Nils is reluctant to leave his business. He goes to church for the first time in ages and begins to wonder if there is something strange about his wife. The couple have an arrangement whereby Nils always strikes his axe three times on an old pine tree near the kiln to give warning of his return. But this time he forgets, and when he reaches the kiln he sees his wife and children busy clearing it out – and they

A charcoal-burner talking to a visiting woman, illustrated by Erik Werenskiold in 'The Charcoal Burner', 1879.

all have bushy tails! Nils goes back to the tree and strikes with his axe; when he returns, everything seems in order. Nils now plots to rid himself of his troll family. Advised by a wise man, he saddles his horse with no loops attached to either saddle or bridle and takes the family out in his sledge onto the lake-ice. There he abandons them to a pack of wolves. Their cries for mercy fall on deaf ears and their calls for help from their troll-kindred fail, for there are no loops that the other trolls can seize to pull the family to safety. Nils sells his charcoal business, retreats to his farm and, although he lies sick for a good few weeks and a shot fired by the trolls damages his stable, he stays there quietly until his death. To us, this story sounds both cruel and exploitative. Nils was happy to make money through his wife's labour; his willingness to kill his children because of his sudden fear of his wife's otherness suggests a stony heart. In many folktales, however, trolls are identified with the demonic; to cohabit with them could put one's own salvation at risk and Nils's change of heart while in church suggests he has suddenly perceived his family as malevolent creatures ultimately bent on his destruction.

In a similar tale from Norway, a troll-woman woos and marries a Christian man. Although she is very ugly, her family give her a fine dowry; at the instant the couple are joined in church her troll-tail falls off, signalling that she is now part of the community. Everything prospers in the home, but the husband grows sick of her and begins to mistreat her. The wife bears everything with patience. One day her husband's horse throws a shoe and he has to make a new one. His wife follows him into the forge and remarks that he is no good as a farrier – he cannot make a shoe

An 1854 illustration by Adolph Tidemand of a typical Norwegian peasant wedding.

that fits. She seizes a red-hot shoe from the anvil, bends it to fit the horse, and the husband attaches it. 'You are very strong,' he remarks. 'Yes,' she says, 'but I would never use my strength against you.' And from that day on, he becomes a model husband, suitably frightened into good behaviour. The troll-woman has assimilated to human society; although she does not leave all her troll characteristics behind, she suppresses her savagery and sets her husband a powerful example. Supernatural female creatures, who are otherwise doomed to damnation, can gain salvation if they can find a man who will marry them and maintain the marriage for the rest of their lives; this is a common story-type in European folk-tradition. The marriage sacrament transforms the troll-woman into a more regular Christian woman with a hope of heaven.

Male trolls are amorous too; they often drop by shielings, the mountain huts in the summer pastures where girls do dairy-work, to woo the herd-girls. No one wants to marry a troll, though, so the creatures resort to subterfuge. In one tale, a girl is up at the shieling and her fiancé comes to visit. She's delighted to see him, but something doesn't feel quite right. And the dog reacts badly to him, growling and bristling and eventually running off. The fiancé declares that he loves the girl so much that he's decided they must marry immediately, and soon splendidly dressed wedding guests from the village are trooping in, bearing delicious food and wonderful gifts, along with a lovely bridal gown and the traditional bridal crown. The dog runs to the real fiancé's house in the village and alerts him to the strange goings-on at the shieling. He races up there, peers through a knot-hole in the wall and sees the guests, the feast and his fiancée, in all her bridal finery. He fires his gun over the roof, and the door flies open; balls of grey yarn roll out from the interior and away down the hillside (this is a typical troll disguise). When he goes inside, the silverware is still lying on the table, but all the splendid food has turned into moss, toadstools, frogs and toads. When he asks the girl why she was sitting there in her crown and gown, she retorts that he surely knows since he's been with her all afternoon, talking about the wedding. It takes a while for the troll-enchanted girl to recover her wits, but to ward off further troll-machinations, the young couple marry as soon as they can – no point in letting a good bridal crown and all the fine bridal ornaments go to waste!

Troll Builders

Some trolls generously offer to build churches or other structures uncannily quickly, in return for a prodigious reward; one such story is told of Kalundborg church on the Danish island of Sjælland. In the twelfth century, the famous crusader and royal councillor, Esbern Snare, resolved to build a splendid church, and a passing troll offered his services. His condition is that if, by the time the church is finished, Esbern has not found out the troll's name, the troll will take Esbern's heart and eyes as his reward. The church rises with amazing speed, and Esbern becomes extremely anxious. When only half of one pillar remains to be erected, Esbern flings himself down in despair on the slope of Ulshøj hill. From underground he hears a voice lulling a baby to sleep: 'Lie still, my baby! Tomorrow your father Fin comes home, and he will give you Esbern Snare's eyes and heart to play with.' Esbern rushes back to the church where the troll is working and shouts 'Fin!' The troll is so furious he hurls the remaining stone in the air, leaving the church with one incomplete pillar. A similar story is told of Lund cathedral in southern Sweden, where St Lawrence was overseeing the construction project. This time the troll (or giant in some versions) demands the sun and the moon on fulfilment of the contract if the saint cannot discover his name. St Lawrence overhears the troll's wife just in time and thus thwarts Finn the troll just as he was placing the last stone in the crypt. The troll and his family try to shake the cathedral to pieces, but, through the power of God, they are turned into stone and in fact Finn can be seen in the crypt to this very day.

The 'guess my name' condition is familiar from the Brothers Grimm story 'Rumpelstiltskin' or the Suffolk tale of 'Tom Tit Tot'; in both, it's a matter of luck that the supernatural being's name is discovered just in time. Knowing something's true name gives you power over it in many belief systems; thus, malign supernatural entities usually try to hide their identities when it comes to making bargains with humans. In one Icelandic tale, a lazy wife is hopeless at spinning and weaving wool into homespun and is delighted when a kindly old woman comes by the farm and offers to take the wool away and do the job for her. All she asks in return is that the wife be able to guess her name in three guesses. The wife eventually confesses what she has done to her husband, who reckons if she can't guess the name the troll will take her. Luckily, one day the husband is up in the mountains where he hears a noise coming from a cave and peers inside. There is a troll-woman at a loom, singing a little song to herself: 'Hi, hi and ho, ho; Gilitrutt is my name.' Thus, the wife saves herself when the troll, now looking much less friendly, returns with the homespun; the troll vanishes on hearing her name, and the wife mends her ways, becoming diligent and working her own wool ever after, as good housewives should. The moral of these 'Rumpelstiltskin'-type stories is that you should not make false claims about your abilities; you should fulfil the duties that you are expected to perform, and not subcontract them. And, we might add, that if something seems too good to be true, it will probably turn out to be a bad bargain in the end.

'Finn the Troll' pillar in the crypt of Lund cathedral, Sweden.

DANGEROUS TROLLS

As noted, trolls vary enormously in size. Norwegian trolls tend to be very large indeed, lumbering through the forests or mistakeable for mountains. When Sir George Dasent translated a selection of Asbjørnsen and Moe's Norwegian tales into English in 1859, his book introduced trolls to the English-speaking world. A series of comic tales about animals forms part of the collection: 'The Three Billy Goats Gruff' became the best known and best loved in the whole book. In that tale, the menacing troll lurks under the bridge and is tricked into letting the first two goat brothers pass across. Each recommends that the troll wait to devour their older and more substantial brother, coming next. The third (and largest) Billy Goat Gruff pokes out his adversary's eyes with his horns, then tears him apart, marrow and bones, and tosses him in the river. Victory over the troll is achieved through brute force, but it is thanks to the younger goats' remarkably quick thinking.

An angry troll causes a landslide in Christian Skredsvig's 1896 painting.

Troll Kidnappers

Trolls are the agents in northern stories that, in the British Isles, are usually told about fairies. In British folklore it's assumed that people who vanish in the wilderness have got caught up in a fairy-dance or been enticed into the other world; but in the north, particularly Iceland, night-prowling trolls are thought to be the ones who make off with campers in the wilds. The autumn sheep round-up that happens high in the mountains is a good opportunity for the trolls. A couple of stories tell how a man vanishes at the round-up. His friends encounter him at the same place the following year. He says that he cannot go home with his former companions; when asked what he believes in, he replies 'the Holy Trinity.' When they meet him again the following year, he has grown rather hairy and stout, reporting, without much conviction, that he believes in God. In the third year, however, he has become completely hairy and, like a troll, is blue-black in colouring. When asked about his faith, he growls, 'I believe in *truntum*, *runtum* and my trolls in the cliffs.' He is now so far gone into the power of the demonic trolls that he can no longer utter the words 'Trinity' or 'God' – a sure sign of damnation in Icelandic folktales.

The bridge-troll spots one of the Three Billy Goats Gruff, illustrated by Otto Sinding in 1896.

The clever girl keeps the night-troll talking until dawn in this painting by Ásgrmur Jónsson, *c.*1950–55.

Trolls and Christianity

Trolls are unusually active at Christmas; the birth of Jesus seems to provoke them, and they delight in ruining people's celebrations. We saw earlier how the trolls that Grettir killed in the north of Iceland struck only on Christmas Eve. Another Icelandic tale, 'The Night-Troll', tells of a troll who would attack a farm when folk went off to church on Christmas Eve; whoever stayed behind to watch the property would be found dead or mad the next day. One brave

A troll turned into a mountain by the sun in an 1896 painting by Christian Skredsvig.

girl offers to take on the task, sitting in the main room with a baby on her lap. Something comes to the window and says, 'I think your hand is lovely, my quick, sharp girl, and *dilly-do*.' The girl retorts, 'It's never cleared up filth, my prowling Kári [a personal name], and *korri-ro*.' The interloper praises her eyes and feet in a similar vein. She replies that her eyes have never looked at evil, nor have her feet trodden in muck. The troll notes that day is dawning in the east; it is too late for him to get home. The girl declares he

The troll-mother wanders among human dwellings and develops a taste for bacon and coffee, in the tale 'When Mother Troll Took in the King's Washing', illustrated by John Bauer in 1914.

must stay in the farmyard and harm no one, for now he is turned to stone. When folk return from evensong, there is a big boulder in the yard that was not there before. As in other troll tales, the rising sun proves fatal, particularly so, perhaps, on Christmas Day when Christ is born.

One Icelandic tale tells of a farmer called Gissur who sets off up the valley with some packhorses to fetch wood. As he rides along, he hears a voice from the eastern side of the river call, 'Lend me your cauldron, sister, so I can boil a man in it.' 'Who is he?' replies a voice from the western side. 'Gissur from Lækjarbotnar', says the first. Terrified, Gissur chooses his best two horses and flees down the valley with the troll-woman closing in on him. One horse dies of exhaustion and he leaps onto the other, arriving at the church just in the nick of time to dash inside. The troll-woman is hot on his heels. As he frantically tolls the church bells, she vanishes – either back up the valley or sinking into the ground – never to be seen in those parts again. Traditional tales assume that all humans are Christian and thus the church can save people from attack by trolls, demons or other supernatural visitants. Some stories relate that the trolls decide to move away from their long-established habitats when a church is built; they can't bear the sound of the church bells.

Elsa Beskow's story from 1914, 'When Mother Troll Took in the King's Washing', relates the efforts of a couple of trolls to live side by side with the humans who have arrived in the neighbourhood. The troll-mother makes her living by becoming the king's laundress, earning money and spending it on tasty human food. But she and her son can't resist stealing some of the princess's little gowns for her son's future children. Inga, a castle servant, is suspected of the theft, expelled from the palace and ends up taking refuge with the washerwoman and her son. One day, she realises that her hosts are both trolls and laundry-thieves and she runs away.

Meanwhile, the troll-son is apprehended mid-theft and the queen now repents of her earlier accusation of Inga. The queen's page finds Inga wandering in the forest and they return to court and marry. The troll family give up their laundry-business and move north, though not before dropping off the stolen baby clothes for Inga's child. Trolls and humans cannot coexist, even when the creatures make an effort to assimilate, the story suggests, for trolls can never properly understand human morality and will always be tempted to take what isn't theirs.

Trolls and Changelings

In Denmark, trolls are the villains in changeling stories. When a couple have a beautiful baby who suddenly fails to thrive, begins to cry all the time and looks ugly and wizened, it's because the trolls have stolen the human baby and replaced it with one of their own. Changelings can be compelled to leave and the trolls made to return the stolen child: if the changeling can be tricked into revealing its identity, then it must go home. The changeling has to be astonished by something; in one tale the suspicious couple roast whole piglets on the hearth, encased in clay. The changeling is so surprised to see 'a sausage that has ears, eyes and a tail' that he says he has never seen anything like it, though he has seen a local forest cut down and regrow three times – a sure sign of living unnaturally long. Now the child has admitted its changeling identity, it can be beaten and thrown outside; the troll-folk will bring back the lost human and reclaim their own. In another tale, also

The troll-mother and her son carry their troll kettle in 'When Mother Troll Took in the King's Washing', illustrated by John Bauer, 1914.

found in the British Isles, the changeling baby is placed on a long shovel and threatened with being put in the bread-oven, a threat that brings its true mother running. Typically, the troll-mother will retort that she has treated the human baby much better than the humans have her infant, but the returned child often does not live for long after its time among the trolls.

In the Swedish writer Helena Nyblom's 1913 story, 'The Changelings,' a baby princess is stolen by a troll-father who thinks she looks adorable, and his own baby troll-daughter is placed in the princess's cradle. Neither mother is happy about the situation; though the fathers love their strange children the mothers remain alienated and suspicious. Black Eyes, the troll-princess, is wilful and bad-tempered, frightening her supposed father; Bianca Maria, the little princess, is good and kind. By the time they are seventeen, both girls are set to be married; the troll-princess to a handsome duke and Bianca Maria to the troll-crown prince. Both realise that they must run away to avoid this fate. Their paths almost cross as each makes her way back to her true home, to be warmly welcomed by her delighted mother, and each marries the other's intended, achieving lasting happiness. This retooling of the changeling story provides both a happy ending and a testament to maternal love and instinct, as well as emphasising the importance of blood: a troll cannot truly be socialised into becoming a princess, nor a princess learn to be a troll.

The lovely princess, Bianca Maria, walks with her adoptive troll family in 'The Changelings', illustrated by John Bauer in 1913.

EW

Man-Eating Trolls

Trolls are not usually subtle creatures. The huge Norwegian trolls can be heard crashing through the forest when they confront the humans in their territory. They also tend to sniff very loudly through their enormous noses, scenting out their prey, for 'the blood of a Christian man' gives off a powerful aroma, just as it does for giants in such British folktales as 'Jack and the Beanstalk.' In some Norwegian stories, when the hero conceals himself in the troll's lair in order to rescue an abducted princess, the troll senses his presence. In the tale 'Lillekort,' young Lillekort hides when the troll returns, biding his time to put his plan into operation, but the troll sniffs him out: 'I smell the blood of a Christian man,' he growls. The princess quickly assures him that he's right; a passing bird dropped the leg of a Christian down the chimney earlier. The princess has got rid of it, she reports, but the smell lingers. Lillekort now steps forward, revealing himself to be a skilled brewer and, with a whole crowd of trolls recruited to assist, he brews up a mighty malt ale for a troll feast. But the ale is so strong that, after drinking it, 'they fell dead like flies.' This is the second princess that Lillekort has rescued from trolls; they are two sisters and both want to marry him. He loves the younger princess. Luckily Lillekort has a twin brother whom he can summon in cases of dire need by shouting extremely loudly three times. He calls for his twin and when he arrives they switch clothes; consequently the older princess rudely

Ash Lad ambushes a three-headed troll in this 1884 illustration by Erik Werenskiold.

elbows her younger sister aside in her haste to fling her arms round the wrong brother's neck. Lillekort gets his heart's desire, the younger princess, and half the kingdom, while his brother is well satisfied both with his bride and the other half of the kingdom.

Trolls will eat whatever they can get hold of, often stealing a poor family's only goat or cow. But, as we know, they particularly like to eat humans. The male hero is the person most at risk; kidnapped princesses remain uneaten so that they can keep the troll's house and do chores. Ash Lad is the hero of many Norwegian stories; the youngest son in a poor family, he loafs around in the ashes on the hearth before showing his true cleverness and courage. In one story Ash Lad takes up employment at a royal palace near a lake. On the other side of the lake lives a troll with some splendid possessions. Ash Lad steals the troll's seven silver ducks and magnificent coverlet. His envious older brothers then tell the king that Ash Lad has boasted that he can steal the troll's golden harp. This is a much riskier and more complicated enterprise, but Ash Lad, as ever, sets off well prepared, with a nail, a birch twig and a candle-stump. The troll grabs him and commands his daughter to put him in the sty to be fattened up, anticipating a troll feast when the young man is slaughtered. For eight days, Ash Lad is given his fill to eat and drink; then the troll-daughter comes to check on his condition. 'Give me your little finger', she cries, but Ash Lad sticks the nail through the bars and when she cuts into it she concludes that he's still as hard as iron and not tender at all. After another eight days, she cuts into the birch twig, and reckons he is still too tough. Eight days later still, Ash Lad proffers the candle-stump, and the daughter cries that now he's ready for eating. The troll goes off to summon the guests, and the daughter is told to slaughter and boil the main course. As the daughter sharpens her knife, Ash Lad tells her she's not doing it properly, and so she gives it to him to sharpen. When she agrees to let him test its sharpness by cutting off her braid, he cuts off her head instead. 'Then he boiled half of her and fried the other half and set the food on the table.' Dressed in the daughter's clothes, Ash Lad sits in the corner, refusing to eat, so the troll tells him to fetch the harp to entertain the guests, thus revealing where it can be found. Ash Lad snatches the harp and jumps into the bread-trough that he has been using as a makeshift boat to row across the lake. The troll calls out to him from the bank, identifying him as the serial thief, and asking, 'But didn't I just eat you?' 'No, it was your daughter you ate,' replies Ash Lad and the troll bursts with rage. Now Ash Lad is well placed to marry the king's daughter and take half the kingdom. Although he is almost served up as the centrepiece in a troll feast, Ash Lad gets away with it through luck, cunning and troll stupidity: the troll-daughter really shouldn't have let him sharpen that carving-knife for her and the troll-father should have seen the difference between his own daughter and Ash Lad wearing the dead girl's clothes. The ruse with the nail, stick and candle-stump is reminiscent of Hänsel's deception of the witch in the Brothers Grimm story 'Hänsel and Gretel,' where the short-sighted witch does not realise that her victim is sticking a bone through the cage bars instead of his finger.

Overleaf: Ash Lad flees from the lake with the troll's golden harp bundled on his back, painted by Theodor Kittelsen in 1900.

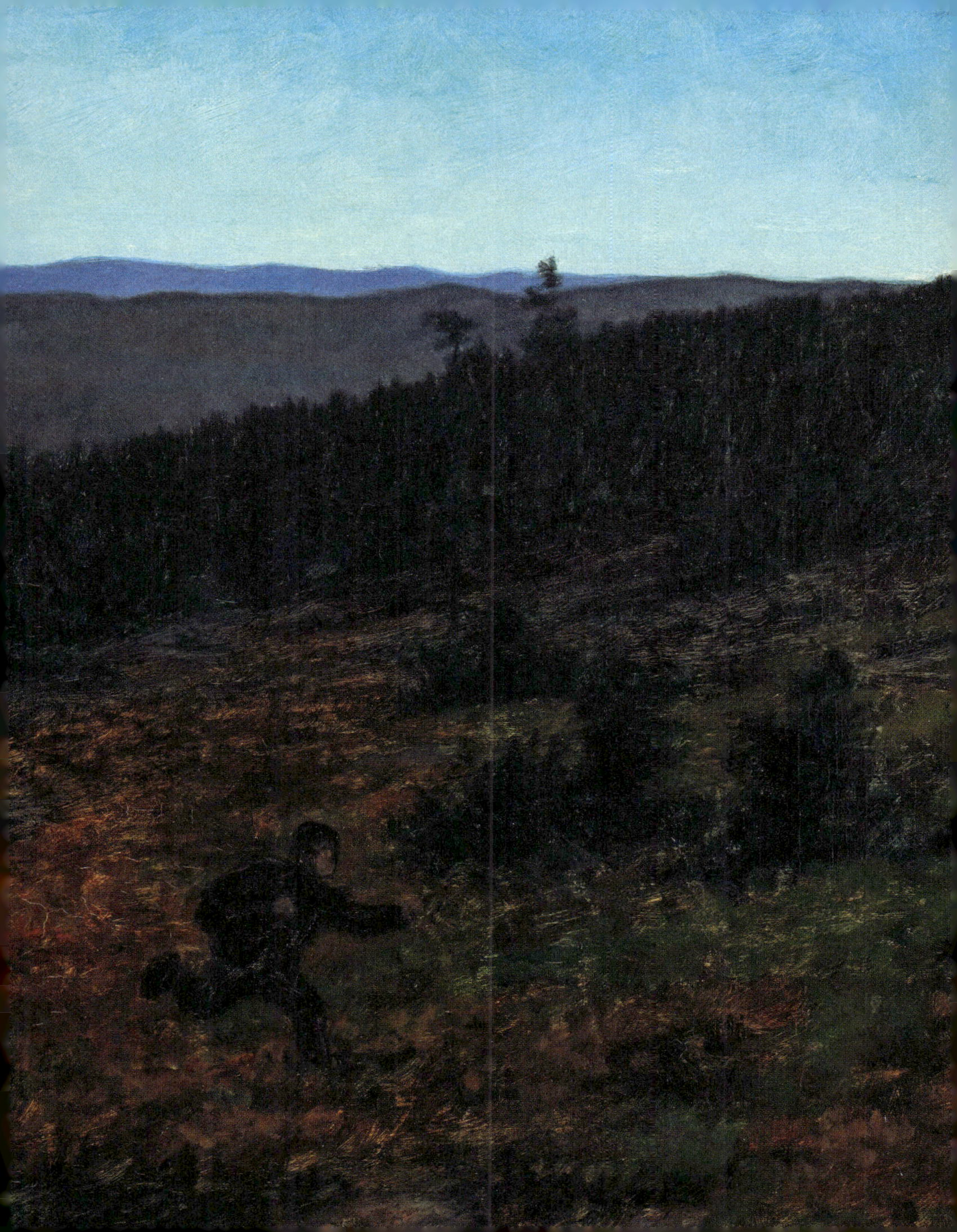

A Girl with a Troll Lover

One long-familiar Norwegian tale, 'The Companion', seems to suggest that a princess might indeed prefer a troll as her lover. In this story, a farm-lad sets out to search for a princess he has dreamed about, but before long he comes to a churchyard where a corpse stands encased in a great block of ice. Everyone spits on it as they go past, and the priest explains that this accursed figure is a vintner who used to water his wine. To the boy, this does not seem a great sin and he pays out of his meagre funds for the dead man to be properly buried. He sets out again and soon acquires a companion who offers to be his servant and pay his own expenses. This story is a long and complex one; the lad and the companion end up winning three vital treasures from three witches: a sword, a ball of golden yarn that can be woven into a bridge, and a magic hat. The witches pursue the two friends to recover the treasures, but eventually are drowned. Now the pair come to the castle where the dream-princess lives and she welcomes the young man, asking him to perform a simple task: keeping her golden scissors for her until the next day. If he doesn't manage to hand them back he will die a horrible death. This seems simple enough, but as the boy and his companion get ready for bed, they discover the scissors are missing. The companion undertakes to look for them. He discovers that the princess has a troll lover whom she visits at night, travelling to his mountain on the back of a billy goat. The witch's hat confers invisibility, so the companion hops up behind the princess and sneaks into the troll's home. There he finds the pair laughing together about the lad's death, and the princess

The princess and her troll lover laughing heartily in Erik Werenskiold's 1886 illustration for 'The Companion'.

entrusts the troll with the scissors. Just as he is placing them in a chest with three iron locks, the invisible companion intervenes and snatches them himself. Thus the scissors are returned to the boy who is able to produce them the following day, to the princess's astonishment. Events repeat themselves, with another ball of golden yarn that the princess entrusts to the young man; it vanishes from his keeping and is recovered from the troll-lair by the companion. On the final day the boy is challenged to bring the princess the thing she is thinking of. During the troll-couple's night-time rendezvous the companion hears the princess say that she will think of her lover's head, surely a quite unguessable answer to her riddle. The princess persuades her lover to escort her home, for the billy goat has been flagging on the return trips, almost as if it were bearing an extra weight. Once the troll has seen the princess safely back to the palace, the invisible companion sneaks up behind him with the magic sword and beheads him. Thus, the next day, when challenged to produce what the princess is thinking of, the lad whips out the troll's head.

Now the boy and the princess are to be married, but the knowledgeable companion reveals that in the bridal chamber he must only pretend to sleep, then seize the bride and strip her of her (hitherto invisible) troll-skin, beating her with birch twigs and scouring her with whey, buttermilk and new milk. The princess comes to the bridal bed armed with a knife to kill her husband, but he overpowers her and removes the enchantment just as the companion prescribed. Then, 'her troll-skin dropped off her and then she was fair, lovely and gentle.' The couple set out for home, the companion carrying the huge dower of gold and silver on his back. When they arrive at the boy's home, the companion bids the couple farewell, saying he will return for half his friend's possessions in five years' time. When he reappears, the treasure is ready and waiting for him, but he also demands half of the couple's child. The father draws his knife ready to keep his promise and kill his boy. The companion now reveals that he is in fact a spirit, the soul of the vintner to whom the man had given burial at the very beginning of the story. He has no need of earthly possessions, nor the child, and the family now live happily ever after. There is a strong Christian moral to this story, in which the boy's instinctive charity is repaid by the dead man, and the biblical story of Abraham and Isaac underlies the tale's coda. The relationship between the troll and the double-dealing princess is both comic and terrifying, its misogyny just about kept in check by the revelation that she has been bewitched and thus is not responsible for her actions.

Norwegian tales are full of abducted and imprisoned princesses and multi-headed trolls who must be slain, often with their own swords, if the women are to be rescued; the famous tale of the troll-castle of Soria Moria is one such. J. R. R. Tolkien took the name of his dwarves' underground kingdom from this glittering castle, a place so far away that Halvor the hero needs the help of the West Wind to find it and rescue the princess imprisoned there.

Not every stolen girl is a princess, of course. A Swedish tale tells how a girl was picking berries on Kusabo mountain when the trolls snatched her. But she wept so much in captivity that they became very annoyed with her and so they threw her back out onto the mountainside. As the mountain closed up, one particularly angry troll dealt her an enormous blow and she was humpbacked for the rest of her life. As in the changeling tales or the story of Johannes Blessom, it is often not possible to survive a troll encounter unscathed; the effects of an encounter with the supernatural linger for the human involved.

Not every girl is a victim. One of the most famous Norwegian tales, 'East of the Sun and West of the Moon', tells of a girl who is given by her father to a polar bear in exchange for riches – a version of 'Beauty and the Beast.' The bear has a splendid castle and at night he sheds his skin and lies down beside the girl in the dark; she is told she must never try to see him. When the girl goes home to visit her parents, her mother persuades her to hide a candle-stump in her clothes so that she can see her mysterious lover. When she lights the candle, she sees that he is indeed the handsomest of princes, spilling three drops of tallow from the candle on her lover's shirt and awakening him. Now she has broken the taboo by looking at him, the bear tells her, the enchantment placed on him by his evil troll-stepmother will not be lifted. He must return to the stepmother's castle, which lies east of the sun and west of the moon, and marry her daughter, a troll-woman with a nose six feet long. The girl undertakes a long journey with many hardships and perils to find him. When she finally arrives at her destination, a castle filled with hideous trolls, the girl needs all her cunning and perseverance to gain access to her lost lover – for the troll-daughter drugs him at night. The girl trades her golden apple and golden carding-comb, treasures she acquired on her travels, for permission to enter the prince's chamber, but he sleeps soundly, despite her

The girl rides on the back of a great white bear, a prince cursed by his troll-stepmother in 'East of the Sun and West of the Moon', by Kay Nielsen, 1922.

KAY NIELSEN 1913

calls and weeping. Finally, she gives the troll-daughter her golden spinning wheel, and that night the suspicious prince does not drink the potion his fiancée offers him. Now the lovers are reunited and hatch a plan to save the prince from his wedding to the troll-bride. The prince produces his shirt with the three spots of tallow and declares he will only wed the woman who can wash them out. This is a task that only Christians can perform, 'not troll riff-raff.' Neither troll-woman is successful in the laundering; their scrubbing makes the spots bigger and blacker. The true bride of course washes the shirt as white as the driven snow and the prince claims her as his beloved. The two troll-women burst with rage and the spell is lifted. The couple leave for home with gold, silver and imprisoned Christian townsfolk, rescued from the troll-castle. This story is a variant on the Greek myth of Cupid and Psyche. It makes the girl into the heroine, the loving woman who is ready to endure endless hardship for her beloved and who gains help from all sorts of creatures and natural forces on her quest to the very ends of the earth.

The Foster-Brothers Silverwhite and Lillwacker

Most of these highly dangerous trolls live in caves in the mountains or roam through the forest. But there are also terrifying sea-trolls who live underwater and rear up to attack ships. In the

Sea-trolls lurk below the waves before rearing up to drown unsuspecting souls in 'The Sea Troll', painted by Theodor Kittelsen in 1881.

Swedish tale, 'Silverwhite and Lillwacker', three sister-princesses are the price demanded by sea-trolls who threaten to capsize their parents' ship. Each princess is escorted to the beach to be handed over by a duplicitous courtier. He has promised to fight for the unhappy girls, but instead runs away and hides up a tree. The hero Silverwhite approaches each princess and promises to defend her; as he lays his head in her lap to have his hair combed she knots a golden ring into his hair. Having earlier been given a sword and three impressive dogs by a paternal figure, Silverwhite kills all three trolls and their ferocious sea-dogs, and he cuts out and pockets the trolls' eyes. The false courtier meanwhile brings each princess home and claims to have overcome the sea-trolls himself, threatening the girls with death if they contradict his story. The courtier's wedding to the youngest princess is in full swing when Silverwhite appears and reveals the truth, proving his valour by displaying the trolls' eyes, while the princesses identify him as their rescuer by the rings they knotted into his hair.

The three sea-trolls turn out to have a brother, while Silverwhite has a faithful foster-brother, Lillwacker. The brothers had separated earlier, and Lillwacker is in service at a king's court not far from the crossroads where they parted. Before he rode on, Silverwhite had drawn runes in the spring at the crossroads and told his foster-brother that if ever the water runs red, Lillwacker will know that his brother is in dire trouble. The final troll-brother manages to kill Silverwhite and when Lillwacker sees that the spring-water has turned red, he sets out in search of his brother. He comes to Silverwhite's castle, and since the foster-brothers look identical, he is taken for Silverwhite. He conceals his true identity while he tries to ascertain what is going on. Thus he spends the night sleeping on a couch in Silverwhite's wife's chamber. During the night the murderous troll-brother knocks on the window and calls him outside.

Lillwacker overcomes the sea-troll in battle and so the creature tries to buy his life with two magical flasks. One contains a useful liquid that can revive the dead and the other has a strong adhesive effect. Lillwacker anoints a stone with the second liquid and the sea-troll sticks fast to it until dawn. The evil creature is thus destroyed by the sun. Silverwhite is revived with the aid of the first magic flask but, unexpectedly, he turns on his foster-brother and kills him for he believes that Lillwacker has spent the night with Silverwhite's wife. It is only when Silverwhite's wife asks her husband why he behaved so oddly the previous night, in refusing to share her bed, that he realises his error: Lillwacker was faithful and true to his brother. Silverwhite quickly revives Lillwacker with the restorative liquid. He marries one of the other princesses and they live in good fortune for the rest of their days.

This tale combines a number of well-known folktale motifs: the false hero who tries to steal the credit for the true hero's deed; the troll turned to stone by the sun; the faithful foster-brother who saves his friend; the fidelity test (spending a night with someone's wife without sharing her bed); and the idea that just when a happy ending seems to be in sight, it turns out that there is yet another troll bent on vengeance, who has to be overcome.

STUPID TROLLS

Ash Lad's Adventures

Usually, trolls are easily outwitted by the smart hero. Asbjørnsen and Moe's stories include tales of stupid trolls who fall for the simplest tricks performed by the hero. Ash Lad frightens one malevolent troll by demonstrating his strength. He claims his grip is so strong that he can squeeze water out of a stone, but what he has in his hand is a bag containing cheese, from which the whey runs down. Impressed, the troll invites him home and challenges him to an eating competition. Ash Lad puts his leather bag on his lap and makes sure to ladle more porridge into it than down his throat. After a while he draws his knife and makes a slit in the bag: porridge oozes out. The troll has been eating a good deal and now feels quite stuffed; he has no room for any more, he says. Ash Lad urges him to do what he has just done: make a slit in his stomach with his knife to relieve the pressure. The foolish troll does exactly that and perishes from the wound. Persuading trolls to play

Ash Lad uses whey and a cheese to make the troll think he can squeeze water from a stone in Theodor Kittelsen's 1883 illustration.

TK.

blind man's buff and making them fall into a lake and drown, or challenging them to a stone-throwing competition in which the hero throws a bird instead of a rock, are also effective anti-troll strategies, either killing them off or impressing them so much that they decide to leave the human in peace.

Marrying a Troll

Like the stepmother in 'East of the Sun, West of the Moon,' troll-mothers are delusional about their ugly offspring's charms and are keen to marry them off to humans. In Walter Strenström's story from 1915, 'Äventyret' (The Adventure), a proud troll-mother shows off her hideous offspring to an unhappy princess who is required to marry one of them. Now they are old enough to marry, the troll-mother ill-advisedly reveals to her sons the magic rhyme that can destroy trolls, but only if uttered by a boy unafraid of darkness or trolls. As it happens, the sons have met just such a boy in the forest, seeking for adventure; he is the son of the castle gatekeeper and has followed the trolls home. Lurking at their window, he overhears the rhyme so rashly revealed by their mother and boldly recites it back to the family. Consequently, the doting mother and her boys are whisked away by the wind, never to be seen again; the boy and princess take the trolls' treasure back to the castle where of course they marry.

Ash Lad tricks a troll into playing blind man's buff, by Theodor Kittelsen, 1906.

In John Bauer's 1913 illustration for 'The Adventure', a proud mother troll tells the kidnapped princess to admire her sons.

Opposite: Erik Werenskiold's 1878 illustration for 'The Lads Who Met the Trolls in Hedal Woods' depicts the trolls who share a single eye between them.

In 'The Lads Who Met the Trolls in Hedal Woods', two brothers are overtaken by night in the forest. It's late autumn and they build a little hut out of pine branches. Then they hear a sniffing and a snuffling, and: 'I smell the blood of a Christian man.' Three enormous trolls are towering above the fir trees, but they only have one eye between them, which slots into a hole on the front of the head. The lead troll has the eye, while the others follow, all holding on to one another. The younger brother runs off and the trolls pursue him. Meanwhile, the elder brother nips behind with his axe and slashes the final troll in the ankle. The troll lets out a horrible shriek, which makes the lead troll start so much that the eye drops out of his forehead. The lad picks it up. The trolls threaten him; if he doesn't return the eye, they'll turn him and his brother into stocks and stones. But these threats have no purchase, since the eye gives out such light the boy can now see very well, and he issues a counter-threat: unless they do what he says, he'll simply continue to cut lumps out of them. Now they offer gold, silver and whatever he wishes, in return for the eye. The boy agrees that one of them may go home and fetch treasure and two good crossbows. The trolls can't see to find their way home, so they begin to shout. Their mother answers and soon she turns up with two buckets of gold and silver and the weapons. Though she blusters and curses the boys, she hands over everything and, with their eye restored to them, the troll party heads off north, never to be heard of again in Hedal Woods.

The Trolls of Dovrefjell

The trolls of Hedal Woods are not exactly stupid, but their disability makes it easy to outwit them, and trolls are quite good, at least, at realising when they simply cannot win. In another tale, set on Dovrefjell (Dovre mountain), a notorious haunt of trolls, a man who has been hunting in the far north and has captured a polar bear stops for the night at a farm. The farmer, Halvor, says he can't offer him shelter, for it is Christmas Eve and every year so many trolls descend on the farmhouse that everyone has to move out. The man says he will manage, so the farmer sets out all kinds of delicious, seasonal food for the trolls and takes off. Soon a rabble of trolls turns up, big, small, with and without tails, and most with exceptionally long noses. As they tuck into the food a troll-child roasting a sausage on the fire notices the bear. 'Hello, tabby cat, do you want some sausage?' it calls and holds the sausage so close to the bear's nose that it is burned. The bear leaps up growling and chases all the trolls out of the house. Man and bear have a peaceful night. Next year, Halvor the farmer is cutting wood in preparation for Christmas when he hears a voice from deep in the forest. 'Hey, Halvor,' it calls, 'do you still have that tabby cat at home?' Halvor thinks quickly, 'Yes! And she's had seven kittens, each even bigger and worse-tempered than their mother.' 'Then we're never coming back to your house,' shouts the troll, and ever after Halvor enjoys Christmas in peace. Once again, the trolls try to wreck Christmas for good Christians.

Overleaf: John Bauer's 1913 illustration of trolls on their way to their Christmas-feast at Halvor's farmhouse.

A version of 'The Tabby Cat of Dovrefjell' is also told about Peer Gynt, the legendary trickster figure who is expert at confounding trolls. He is a great marksman – trolls hate being shot at and usually run away from guns. He can also decode trolls' riddling language and see through their shape-changing tricks. Henrik Ibsen's play *Peer Gynt* (1867) incorporates many folklore motifs, including of course the famous trolls, made particularly vivid through Edvard Grieg's incidental music. After running away up into the mountains with Solveig, daughter of a religious family, Peer comes to a shieling where the dairymaids are expecting some trolls to come and court them. They all get very drunk, and next day a hungover Peer hits his head on a rock. What follows may thus be a hallucination. The troll-king's green-garbed daughter brings him to her father's hall where many trolls are assembled. The troll-king (the Dovregubben, as he is called in Norwegian) offers to transform Peer into a troll if he will marry his daughter. Various conditions are set for the match, and Peer finally declines. The troll-king explains the difference between trolls and humans. Humans say, 'Man, be yourself' – that is, be humane and empathetic – but trolls say, 'Troll, be sufficient unto yourself' and they don't need to care about anyone else. Peer now adopts this egotistical credo and leaves the mountain to go on further adventures. In the play's final act, towards the end of Peer's life, the troll-king reappears and declares that Peer has indeed been a troll, not a human, for most of his life. Like their folkloric relatives, Ibsen's trolls symbolise self-centredness and uncaring individualism; they pay no heed to the needs or feelings of others. Instead, they simply take what they want, shun general social morality and pay no regard to the impact they might have on the larger community.

Peer Gynt is brought to the Hall of the Mountain King by the King's daughter, illustrated by Arthur Rackham in 1936.

The Trolls

TROLLS, MODERN AND CONTEMPORARY

Trolls in Fantasy Novels

Through Dasent's 'The Three Billy Goats Gruff,' Ibsen's drama, *Peer Gynt*, and Grieg's hypnotic music for the play, including the rollicking 'In the Hall of the Mountain King,' trolls became internationally famous. In the twentieth century they emerge as a staple of fantasy. J. R. R. Tolkien includes in *The Hobbit* three comedy Cockney trolls who, as tradition demands, turn to stone as the sun rises. More sinister and terrifying troll-like figures, the evil Orcs and the Uruk-Hai, all creatures of Sauron, rampage through *The Lord of the Rings*. In the Harry Potter books, Hermione has a close shave with a troll when she misses a troll-alert that warns the other children that one is loose in the school. This troll is a classic Scandinavian creature: huge, lumbering and vicious. It corners

Tolkien's own illustration of Gandalf approaching the three trolls who have kidnapped Bilbo and the dwarf company in *The Hobbit*, 1937.

Hermione in a Hogwarts bathroom and it is only thanks to Ron's levitation spell that she and Harry survive the attack.

Trolls are found in Terry Pratchett's Discworld universe too, where they are essentially animated rocks; in the early books they are regarded as stupid and dangerous, but later in the series they become increasingly civilised. They are still largely nocturnal (too much sunshine can make their brains overheat), but they tend not to eat humans any longer. Some, indeed, have become useful citizens in the capital, Ankh-Morpork, joining the City Watch where their willingness to work by night and their lingering propensity for violence come in useful. Moomintroll and his family, the creations of the Finnish writer Tove Jansson, are not particularly trollish. Moomintroll himself is the only troll in the book series; yet the inclusion of the -troll element in the English version of his name has helped to make trolls lovable. The popular children's toys were invented in Denmark in the 1950s by Thomas Dam, and soon became a worldwide phenomenon, with their wide-set eyes, ugly but cute snub noses (not the traditional long snouts for sniffing out Christians with) and their brightly coloured shock of hair. In 2013, the media company DreamWorks licensed the troll concept from Dam and now three troll movies have been produced, complemented by TV specials and spin-off animations – and a good deal of associated merchandise.

Tove Jansson's illustration of Moomin and friends on the 2019 Swedish edition cover of *Trollkarlens Hatt* (Finn Family Moomintroll).

A troll in the 2010 Norwegian found-footage, folk-horror film *Trolljegeren* (Troll Hunter).

The cinema poster for DreamWorks' 2023 animation, *Trolls Band Together*.

Movie Trolls

In the adult world, the 2010 Norwegian film *Trolljegeren*, in English Troll Hunter, is a folk-horror comedy; like *The Blair Witch Project*, it purports to be found footage. A group of students falls in with a troll-hunter and discover that many kinds of troll still exist in the Norwegian wilderness. The troll-hunter works for a government agency that aims to contain trolls, eliminating any who come too close to human settlements. The film utilises many folkloric conceptions: there are gags about the trollish ability to 'smell the blood of a Christian man,' goats crossing a bridge are used as bait, and the troll-hunter is armed with a UV weapon that mimics sunlight. In the Norwegian monster comedy *Troll* from 2022, the Mountain King himself is awakened when a new railway is built through Dovrefjell. The troll goes on the rampage, marching on Oslo where his palace had once stood. Christians massacred his family and now he seeks vengeance. Off he tramps down Karl Johans Street, as in a famous illustration by Theodore Kittelsen, terrifying everyone in sight. Loudly ringing church bells and all the sunbeds in Oslo are deployed against the troll and the use of nuclear weapons is contemplated, but finally the rising sun on a (rare) cloudless day turns the unhappy creature into stone.

The lead character in the Oscar-nominated Swedish film *Gräns* (Border) from 2018, by the Iranian director Ali Abbasi, is Tina, an unusual-looking customs officer who can smell human emotions and who is strangely drawn to a regular traveller from Finland, Vore, who seems very much like her. Tina discovers that trolls still exist, can pass among humans, and were systematically mistreated by humans in the 1970s in Sweden. A few trolls have survived in Finland. Vore is seeking vengeance for humans' past brutality, a subplot involving changeling troll-babies. Tina discovers the truth about her own origins and has to decide where her true loyalties lie. Addressing many of the same questions raised a hundred years or more ago in *Peer Gynt*, the film asks probing questions about difference and diversity, acceptance and individualism.

CHR MAGNUS

Online Trolls

The internet troll's name probably derives from a long-established verb: *to troll*, which has multiple meanings related to movement. At times it has meant, 'to wander about', 'to pass from hand to hand', 'to sing in a round', or 'to trawl', throwing out a fishing-net to see what can be caught. It is probably this final meaning that gave rise to the idea of online trolling: throwing out erroneous or hostile comments to see who takes the bait. The *Oxford English Dictionary* records this sense for the verb from as early as 1992. The internet troll as noun is also recorded from this year. The *Dictionary* suggests that the folkloric figure has now fused with the modern concept: a creature that lurks menacingly in the dark, one that is not very bright and is bent on malice.

Trolls have escaped from the black lava wastes of Iceland and the dense pine forests of Scandinavia to take on a new life in the collective global imagination. They may not steal goats and eat people quite so much, but they remain disruptive and dangerous, even if their limited imaginations sometimes make them comic and even quite likeable. They can be neutralised and outwitted, though they never disappear for good. The troll is always out there, patrolling the edges of human culture and ethics, ready for its next incursion.

Theodor Kittelsen's 1892 illustration of a troll tramping down Karl Johans Street in Oslo is recreated in the 2022 Norwegian film *Troll*.

Picture Credits

1 Nationalmuseum Sweden; **2** National Museum of Art Norway; **6** Norske Folkesmuseum; **9** National Museum of Norway; **10-11** National Museum of Norway. Photo Nasjonalmuseet/Andreas Harvik; **12**, **14** British Library; **15** Private Collection; **16** © Brian Froude; **21** Árni Magnússon Institute for Icelandic Studies; **25** Árni Magnússon Institute/Bridgeman Images; **26** © John Vernon/The Folio Society; **30**, **32** National Museum of Norway. Photo Nasjonalmuseet/Ivarsøy, Dag Andr; **34**, **35** Private Collection; **38-9**, **41** National Museum of Norway. Photo Nasjonalmuseet/Ivarsøy, Dag Andre; **43** National Library of Norway; **47** steve789/123RF.com; **48** National Museum of Norway. Photo Nasjonalmuseet/Andreas Harvik; **50** British Library; **52** Listasafn Íslands, Safn Ásgríms Jónssonar/National Gallery of Iceland, Collection of Ásgrímur Jónsson, LÍÁJ 311 Ljósmyn /Photograph: Listasafn Íslands/National Gallery of Iceland/SG; **53** National Museum of Norway. Photo Nasjonalmuseet/Andreas Harvik; **54**, **57** Private Collection; **59** Nationalmuseum Sweden; **60**, **64-5**, **67** National Museum of Norway. Photo Nasjonalmuseet/Ivarsøy, Dag Andre; **71** British Library; **73** National Museum of Norway. Photo Nasjonalmuseet/Høstland, Børre; **76**, **78** National Museum of Norway. Photo Nasjonalmuseet/Ivarsøy, Dag Andre; **80** Nationalmuseum Sweden, **81** National Museum of Norway. Photo Nasjonalmuseet/Ivarsøy, Dag Andre; **84-5** Artepics/Alamy Stock Photo: **87** British Library; **88** British Library © Estate of J.R.R. Tolkien; **91** © Tove Jansson (1965), Moomin Characters TM; **92** left AJ Pics/Alamy Stock Photo; **92** right © Universal Pictures/Courtesy Everett Collection; **94** De Kongelige Samlinger Norway.